Ancient
Wisdom I

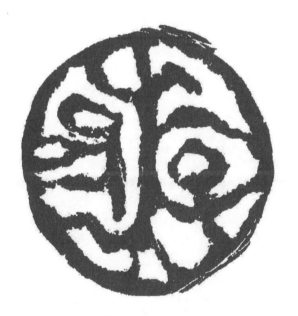

"For Harwood, who makes 'Money Sense'"

Ancient Wisdom I

P. Zbar

The Spiritual Tale of the Scholar Chu Shui Hu

Capital Books, Inc.
Sterling, Virginia

CAPITAL
BOOKS, INC.

Capital Books, Inc.
P.O. Box 605
Herndon, Virginia 20172-0605

ISBN 1-892123-45-2   (alk.paper)

Library of Congress Cataloging-in-Publication Data

Trupp, Philip Z. (Philip Zbar)
  Ancient wisdom I : the spiritual tale of the scholar Chu Shui Hu / P. Zbar.
    p. cm.
  ISBN 1-892123-45-2
  1. Hu, Chu Shui—Anecdotes. 2. Calligraphers—China—Anecdotes. I. Title.

Nk3634.H8224 T78 2001
181′.11—dc21   00-069350

Printed in the United States of America on acid-free paper that
meets the American National Standards Institute Z39-48 Standard.

First Edition

10 9 8 7 6 5 4 3 2 1

*T*o Young Kang, Ph.D., a friend beyond measure whose wisdom and mentoring spirit set this book in motion.

Hu meditates as distant music stirs Zhongnan shan. His caoshu characters remind the listener that patience allows one to hear the music of heaven.

*G*ratitude to Kathleen Hughes, publisher of powerful *qi*, whose vision allowed this work to develop and go forward, and to her colleagues Jane Graf, Kristen Gustafson, Noemi Taylor, Jeanne Hickman, and the gifted designers Suzanne and Kevin Chadwick.

Deepest appreciation to Young Kang, Ph.D., who opened the door to the wonders of the East and lit the way with generosity and kindness; Ling Liu, Chinese language editor of priceless insights; Ben Lee, friend and mentor who never tired of my questions; Kohei Takagaki-Sensei, Japanese master whose inspiration broadened the path and informed the spirit; Xiang Wang, patient Chinese master who revealed bamboo, wren and cricket; Miyuki Myoshikami and family for kindness; Janell Cannon, renowned author/illustrator whose friendship is a treasure; Jay Jagoe for enthusiasm of intellect; Kathy Williams for an eye to Asian culture; Elise Grenier who rescued me from the void; Robin Zhang for revealing greatness in small things; Salman Nensi who enhanced the tools of calligraphy; Helen and Peter Panarites for bridges.

The author also wishes to acknowledge the works of William McNaughton, Kenneth Rexroth, Johan Bjorksten, Dr. Ong Tee Wah, Tan Huay Peng, Richard Wilhelm, J.W. Hackett, Ching Yee, Situ Tan, Chung Po-Ho, Hsueh Wen-yu, Cyril Birch, Amy Tan, Edwin O. Reischauer, John K. Fairbank, J.A.G. Roberts, Stefan Rudnicki, Edoardo Fazzioli, Deng Ming-Dao, Rebecca Hon Ko, Barbara Aria, Russell Eng Gon, Man-Ho Kwok, Martin Palmer, Jay Ramsay, Kowk-Lap Chan, and master Chang-Yi.

To my wife Sandy, deepest respect for patience, love, and sharing the mystery of Hu's adventures.

"Heaven's greatest power is the essence of *qi*."

*T*his is a story about Chinese language and spirit, yet it is much more than a collection of artfully composed characters. It gives us a highly concentrated picture of the charm and beauty of Chinese calligraphy as an art and venue to pursue one's worth. In the time-honored Chinese way, the abstract concepts are revealed through the eyes of a young scholar's self-cultivation in the mythical mountains of Zhongnan Shan. During his long and lonely days and nights in a shabby cabin, he illuminates and interprets the most valued virtues of Chinese culture in a fashion so familiar to this world.

Originated from pictographs on tortoise shells 5,000 years ago, Chinese characters have gradually evolved through all the dynasties into the sophisticated system we know today. The combination of different vowel tones and the huge number of characters make it one of the most complicated, if not the most difficult, language to learn. Yet what makes the written character most fascinating is its dual role as a language and an art.

For the Chinese, the writing brush has also been the brush of the artist. The four treasures of the calligrapher—brush, ink stick, paper, and ink stone—provide what the ancients called "the means of metamorphosis," the tools to express complex emotions and ideas. These artists draw their inspirations from willow branches in the breeze, water falls in the mountains, and even the flying curves of the martial master's sword.

Different artists may follow different styles: *li* (the square, official style); *cao* (the cursive style); *xing* (the running script); *kai* (the standard style). But the beauty of every stroke rendered shows the artist's deep and sincere love of nature and humanity, perseverance in the search of personal perfection or salvation, and the sacrifice of worldly wealth and fame.

For our hero, Chu Shui Hu, the writing brush allows him to become a master of art; but more important, it gives him the selfless joy of finding simplicity and "emptiness of art," the highest reward of self-cultivation that Taoist scholars pursue, especially during the T'ang Dynasty, Hu's period.

To readers like me who were born and raised in China, Hu's story brings back all the nice, warm memories of those tales our mum and grandma told or we read at school: The poor little boy who only had lightning bugs for reading at night but educates himself to be a great strategist; the persistent and modest young man who patiently endures the teasing of the old wide man to become his student; a famous calligrapher who darkens a whole pond by washing his brush while practicing his skills for years in the mountains. Chu Shui Hu reminds me of every one of them and of all of them. Young and talented, these heroes start as nobody and work their way up through perseverance, diligence, modesty, and continuous introspection to realize the true essence of enlightenment.

Real or fictitious, these role models teach us the fundamental values that Chinese culture cherishes and that we still live and breathe in our everyday life. "*Shu shan you lu qin wei jing, xue hai wu ya ku zuo zhou*" (The only way up the mountain of knowledge is diligence, the only boat to cross the endless sea of wisdom is hard work). "*Xu huai ruo gu*" (The greatest scholar has the mind as open as the valley). The familiar context and vivid description of Hu's journey make it easy and comfortable for me to feel great empathy with his ups and downs. I can imagine him meditating and sweating on the scrolls in his little cabin on Zhongnan Shan. I can hear him talking to the moon about his frustrations and determination. Hu's struggle to gain perfection takes the reader on a true spiritual journey.

To those who are not native to the culture, the story provides a very important insight to the Chinese people and their values. When China is no longer isolated from the rest of the world, and while East and West draw closer and closer, effective trans-Pacific communication becomes evermore critical. Won't the interaction be much easier if we gain a broader picture of our cultural values and thus better appreciate each other's view of the world?

It is not enough to know the collectivist label that the East bears and the individualistic prototype of the West. Seeing each other in perspective and understanding the roots of our values and rituals will move us one step closer to learning how many of the lessons taught in this book apply to the benefit of all humankind.

—Ling Liu
University of Maryland
College Park

Breath (*Chi*):
This ancient character also means "air" or "life force." *Chi* is used in the Western world but in China they call it "*qi*." Hu struggled with many brushes and covered much paper before achieving the flowing elegance of this sacred word-symbol.

*I*n the days before tiger smoked, Chu Shui Hu was ordered from the Palace at Ch'ang-an to the mountains of Zhongnan Shan to face a monastic life, a command which came without warning and disturbed the pursuit of his prodigious scholarship.

Why did his patron and master, Xi Er Gong, insist that he take leave of the Palace? Indeed, Hu was a magician of learning. If he often spoke out of turn it was only by impatience to be of service. After all, it was Xi who had sponsored him at the Imperial University and groomed him for a life of scholarly achievement, and for this Hu was deeply grateful.

Anger (*Huo qi*):
A flame reaching upward, sparks on either side (bottom character), combined with air (*qi*), indicating wrath. Anger consumed Hu upon learning he was to be sent to Zhongnan Shan. His ink flies across the paper to score his intensity.

"Now you are to become a calligrapher," Xi told him. "You will devote three years to this challenge."

Three years in Zhongnan Shan seemed an eternity to the headstrong Hu, but to the masters of Chinese calligraphy it was but two blinks of an eye.

Hu's hand had been adequate to pass the Imperial examinations, though his skill was hardly the level required of the imposing "literati," the select monks and ascetics who acted as medusas of the universe, free-spirited wanderers who created magical forms of the word with brush and ink.

To Act (*Wei*):
Once committed, Hu responded to Xi's challenge. Using simplified script indicating strength of purpose (bottom), he created the flowing character (above).

The weight of the undertaking made Hu's head hurt.

"Why me?" he cried. "I have been your earnest scholar, your intellectual servant."

Xi's face darkened.

"Acorns do not argue with the oak," he replied. Hu was to master the calligrapher's brush to compose scrolls of wisdom with the highest aesthetic values. "Biao in li yi. Create a style so fine it will enchant the Emperor," Xi instructed.

"But would it not be better to study with a master at Ch'ang-an?" Hu asked. "Why must I journey to Zhongnan Shan and leave all I have worked for?"

Family (*Shi*):
Hu wondered if he would ever settle down. "Seeds of the water lilly follow the stirring wind," he wrote. "Am I the rootless one?" *Jen*, patient in the face of his self-absorption, responded, "Tao is the wind and water. The seed must know where the rocks are."

Xi raised his hand just as the youth was about to embellish his complaints.

"When you drink water, think of its source," Xi said, turning his back to his sputtering *moshi* scholar.

Hu was obedient. It was a matter of honor. His arrival at the Palace had been a stroke of serendipity. He recalled the day long ago when one of Xi's eunuchs discovered him reading from Confucian texts in the shelter of a bamboo grove.

The eunuch was astonished. How did a peasant boy obtain such rare texts, let alone learn to read them?

Book (*Ce*):

In ancient times, bamboo slips were pieced together to form a scroll or leafs of a book. Hu's simplified character (top) is taken from the seven-stroke pictogram (bottom right). A proverb tells us, "Books do not bow to kings; their allegiance honors learning."

"Curiosity is a poor boy's *qi*," Hu replied, evading the question.

"Poor boys have no scrolls," said the eunuch. "Where is your family?"

"My family is with the *Tao te Ching*, eternal and everlasting."

The eunuch sensed this was no ordinary boy. As a peasant he was merely a frog at the bottom of a well, one who might never see the capitals of Ch'ang-an and Lo-yang, the citadels of the T'ang Dynasty. Yet in an era when art and scholarship were glorious, the discovery of a golden frog was bound to bring much honor.

Literary (*Wen*):
The symbol (bottom right) is borrowed from a two-part sign meaning "Chinese characters." Inspired by nature, Hu invented a new character to indicate the ongoing cycle of literary pursuit.

"You are quick with words," the eunuch told him. "Indeed, you speak in shadows. I have asked you a question, and you are hiding from an answer."

"I have only my mother," Hu said plainly. "My father and brothers were assassinated in the feudal war. My unfortunate mother is blind." He held up his right hand. "As you can see, I am small and my hand was victim to an ox."

Assassins were not sent against the common people. Perhaps Hu's father was a nobleman singled out for death all the way back to the fourth generation, eliminating virtually all living family members.

Chinese Characters (*Wen*): Legend attributes these symbols (below) to Emperor Yu the Great, who discovered the pictograms on the shell of a tortoise in 2200 BC. The modern form (above) emerged from the works of the "literati" who sought to create a more fluid style.

The eunuch suspected the boy was posing as a peasant to save himself and his mother from harm.

The eunuch asked Hu to follow him to a bridge spanning a stream. As they approached the center of the bridge the eunuch removed his shoe, flung it into the water, and ordered him to recover it. Soaking wet, Hu at last returned with the shoe.

"Put it on for me," the eunuch commanded.

Hu knelt and replaced the shoe.

Balance (*Yun*):
The top radical is wind (*feng*); beneath it is water (*shui*). Together they convey the balance of nature, or a suitable place to live. In Hu's composition, wind stirs the water, dominating it and creating lack of harmony.

The eunuch was convinced he had discovered a boy worthy of teaching, the issue of a nobleman who might serve in the ministerial offices of the Palace. Indeed, he wrote to Xi:

> *He is clear of brow, fine of eye*
>
> *White his teeth, red his lip*
>
> *Upright and dignified of step*
>
> *Sharp and quick-witted in speech*
>
> *Beyond the student in intelligence*
>
> *Equal of a grown man in subtlety.*
>
> *A Little Frog beyond price.*

Book of Changes
(*Yi Ching*):
Scholars believe this classic of divination pre-dates the Chou Dynasty (1200 BC). Hu was drawn to the simplicity of archaic forms (*xiang xing*), or "image shapes," to create characters which implied mood. The pictogram "Book" (*ce*) floats above "Moon" (*yue*) to capture the "ever-passing moment."

With Xi's approval, the eunuch returned to Hu's village with orders to bring the boy and his mother to the Palace.

Thus, Hu was rescued from his well of obscurity. The Palace had given him safety. Indeed, he had tasted Xi's Imperial water. Now he must replenish the source.

Rice (*Mi*):

The character depicts the seedling, roots, grains, and leaves and indicates six steps used in the preparation of perfect rice. *Mi* also means "essence" of spirit. *Yi Ching* reminds us: "When rice is mature, it bows."

*T*here was no mule for the long journey.

"One cannot capture tiger cubs without going into the tiger's lair," Xi told him. "It is time to learn that seeing once is better than hearing a hundred times."

Hu traveled many miles and wore out many pairs of sandals. The Mongol barbarians had retreated to the north and he traveled without fear. He conversed freely with the people of the countryside and enjoyed their hospitality. He no longer posed as a peasant boy, the Little Frog. He was a voyager from the capital, an honored guest.

Beautiful (*Mei*):
A combination of sheep and big. As an ideograph, it suggests a mature person of gentle ways. In the thrall of Magu, Hu transformed the ancient symbol (bottom right) in use throughout China today.

With weary legs he passed through farm lands and rested in the villages along the way. In the evenings he meditated with ancient men and local prophets who sought meaning in the flickering of a candle.

Farmers described harvests and rain, and in the terraced hills he was invited to harvest the rice. The paddies were beautiful to see, even if they were cold and disagreeable to the touch. He labored beneath unflinching sun and prayed that his father and brothers were at peace in the Yellow Spring. Why had he survived? Perhaps he would find the answer in the magic mountain.

Ritual Wine
(*Chang*):

In the tradition of master calligraphers, Hu consumed the aromatic "wine of happiness." The pictogram shows a vase of distilled rice canted on its side to convey affects of the wine. Beneath the vase is a ladle for sharing.

*A*t last he reached Zhongnan Shan, realm of spirits and mysteries, its peaks rising above the clouds. He knelt on his mat and lit incense. Night was nearly upon him. He must build a fire and study the texts he had brought from Ch'ang-an. Weariness spread through him like a flood. As night fell, he put away his texts and rested on his mat contemplating the stars sailing across heaven like ships on a black ocean.

Color (*Se*):

In ancient times, color was a combination of man and woman, the glow of their complexions indicating emotion. Hu placed "Sun" (*ri*) above an undulating line to convey the changing colors of nature as the sun travels across the sky.

Hu began his ascent the following morning. The bamboo forests at the base of the mountain were green enigmas designed to bewilder. At night he heard the prowling white tiger. The ancients said that one who sees a white tiger in Zhongnan Shan will never leave the mountain.

Hu was grateful to find his way above the bamboo. The forests gave way to towering waterfalls and cliffs glowing with the fire of emeralds. Boulders and rapids impeded him, and nights without shelter were dangerous.

Mountaintop
(*Shan*):

Mountains resonate with Heaven. Temples are built on the heights. The character with three peaks (far left) rising from Earth has changed only slightly over the ages. Hu struggled to invent a new character, without success. "Indeed, the mountain has a mind of its own," he concluded.

Many days had passed and the sun was disappearing behind the mountain when Hu arrived at his new home: a tumbledown bamboo hut shrinking into a forest of pine, as if to hide its poverty. The sight of it filled him with dismay.

It required great will for Hu to bring himself to enter the hut, but as darkness covered the sky and the air grew colder, he sighed and stooped below the narrow lintel.

S n o w (*X u e*):

The character combines rain with the three strokes of broom; rain which may be swept away or taken up by hand (below). Hu preferred the Caoshu image (above).

The glow from his oil lamp was cowed by the darkness. When he stood straight up his head barely escaped the ceiling. Four strides carried him across the interior. *Four*: the unlucky number. Despondent, he dropped his rucksack and spread his mat. Only the whisper of a nearby stream punctuated the gloom. That first night Hu wrote:

> *The thousand sorrows of*
> *this world*
>
> *Arise from parting, in life*
> *or by death....*

Root (*Ben*):

The pictogram shows a tree with a low horizontal stroke indicating Earth. The vertical stroke continues downward, symbolizing root. The root is the lowest part of the tree, said Hu's mother, yet its value is beyond measure. Hu's composition is taken from the archaic form at lower right.

*H*e awoke to golden sunlight. The hut had been transformed. To his amazement, a carved rosewood table stood beside his window overlooking the valley. A spray of plum blossoms shaded a large wooden box, and arranged beside it were rolls of white paper distilled from the bark of mulberry trees.

Was he dreaming? Had these gifts appeared out of nowhere? Surely they had not been there the night before.

Hu rubbed his eyes and approached the table. The box contained the tools of calligraphy: the finest ink stone, known as "red silk" carved in the shape of the Manchurian tiger; ink sticks, the "means of

Man (*Ren*):
Working from early pic-
tograms (left), Hu simplified
the image to show a man
standing erect.

metamorphosis" fashioned from the soot of burnt pine and gum and decorated with Taoist motifs and the seal of Li T'ing. Beneath an array of brushes he found a miniature scroll from *The Calligraphic Strategy of Lady Wei*. Her words provided his first lesson:

> *The sheet of paper is the battle-ground; the brush: the lances and swords; the ink: the mind, the commander-in-chief; ability and dexterity: the deputies; the composition: the strategy. By grasping the brush the outcome of the battle is decided: the strokes and lines are the commander's orders; the curves and returns are the mortal blows.*

H e a v e n (*Tian*):
The images are combinations of man, great, and sky. Hu improvised, ink flew from his brush to form splatters: "Visitations of the gods," Hu's trademark "black butterflies." Seeking greater abstraction, he modified *qi*.

Hu felt the weight of his culture as never before. Thousands of years of history and the most sophisticated civilization the world had ever known fell heavily on his shoulders.

"*Biao xin li yi,*" he whispered with a sense of awe. "The path flows from The Highest. I must master the sages and create what has never been seen before."

Hu's mysterious night visitor left behind volumes of instruction on the philosophy and technique of calligraphy as well as fragments from the diaries of the master medusas.

Happiness (*Xi*):
Emotion expressed by musical symbols. The bottom part of the character is a drum on its stand, skin stretched over it. Immediately above is mouth, indicating song. At the top is a hand prepared to strike the drum. Hu removed strips of bark from a mulberry tree, soaked them in ink, and applied them to paper to form his images.

Days and nights Hu studied with great *qi*. He wrote commentaries on the physical and spiritual attributes of Chinese characters. He meditated on the Oracle and Dragon Bones, the prehistoric word-symbols incised on the shoulder blades of oxen and on tortoise shells.

Philosophy, wisdom, prophecy: all bowed to the word. And the word must be a work of art so elegant that it is understood by all. The character denoting the stream beside his window was a simple composition of three curved lines, yet the lines implied a more subtle meaning: the constancy of water seeking the sea.

Laughter (*Xiao*): The character indicates man swaying back and forth in order to laugh more freely. Above man are two elements of bamboo, suggesting that laughter sways with the wind. "How unusual," Hu wrote. "Except for swaying man and the flickering bamboo, the character is very similar to 'beauty'."

Three bold peaks above a flat line was the simple word-symbol for mountain, yet its composition suggested a noble calling: strength, perseverance. Beyond the peaks lay the first word written in Chinese, "Heaven." Indeed, his own heart resembled the written "radical" with its gentle curves and all-seeing "eyes."

Each day Hu meditated as he swirled his black ink stick against the surface of the red silk stone. It was hard work and his hand ached. He mixed the ink shavings with water from the stream. Dark fluid gathered in the well. He positioned sheets of paper on the table and selected

Spirit (*shen*), Essence (*jing*), Breath (*qi*): Elements of self-discipline needed to master the brush. Hu was driven to compose the creed in a way which reflected art-within-art.

a brush. His hand, injured in childhood, trembled as he dipped the bristles. *Courage*, he told himself. *It is time to act*!

He worked diligently to compose copies of the calligrapher's creed: Mastery of essence (*jing*); spirit (*shen*); and breath, the life-giving force (*qi*). But his hand stumbled against his best intentions and mocked him with awkward, inelegant lines. Even the ink mocked him, migrating with a will of its own through the paper to form sloppy gray shapes.

Again and again Hu swirled his ink stick against the stone and dipped his brush. He must ease his breathing and

R a i n (*Yu*):

Four drops fall from the clouds (the open-ended container) drifting in the sky (indicated by the upper horizontal line). Hu sought to convey the power of rain to influence life. The composition derives from a poem, "Clear After Rain," by Tu Fu, of the T'ang.

become one with his instruments so that his spirit might be released. The brushes were old, some barely more than a few strands of animal hair, yet they were magical in the hands of a strong calligrapher.

The Little Frog was not so gifted. Often the simplest characters defied him. Indeed, he was a prodigious scholar, but the brush tested his limits. Reams of paper lay crumpled on the floor as a silent testament to his frustration.

The *Yi Ching* teaches that success comes from the primal depths of the universe if one perseveres in what is right.

Good, to Love (*Hao*):

The compound character reflects moral values. Woman (*nu*, above) is joined by child or son (*zi*, below). Hu composed the characters in reverence for his mother. "Set adrift and impoverished by assassins, she sacrificed her vision sewing garments for others," he wrote. "Her goodness is beyond measure."

Hu's blind mother knew little of the great book, yet the day his father and brothers were taken away in war, she held him and spoke plainly: "As wood draws strength from the root, which is in the lowest place, so the power to rise above adversity grows from the lowest station."

Indeed, he would be strong as the root. He would persevere.

Months passed before Lady Wei's appeal to generalship crystallized in his mind. He had been ordered to a field of battle against his own inadequacy. He must see himself with new eyes. The great

Deep (*Xuan*):
An abstraction of two cocoons beneath a roof, a dark place where silkworms are grown. In early Chinese history, the character indicated the color green. Taoist theories of art redefined green as a per-mutation of black. Hu soon learned that his sooty ink stick yielded many shades, each with a special meaning.

calligraphers of old faced the same challenge. He must strive with increasing effort to release the spiritual forces within him. Calligraphy exemplified inspiration and devotion, a sacred act born of spirit. Indeed, patience was required if the confluence of skill and spirit were to be realized.

Hu practiced the script of the Great Seal (*da zhuan*) and Small Seal (*xiao zhuan*), as well as the Official Form (*li shu*). In more lighthearted moments he composed *fu*, those fanciful talismans of good fortune which decorated the dwellings of the peasants he had met on his journey to

Mysterious

(*Xuan miao*):

A combination of deep and fantastic. Magu said, "Be like the valley which parts to the stream. The valley is at once empty and always filling with mysterious power."

Zhongnan Shan. Pleased by an unrealized talent for design, he gained confidence.

One morning Hu awoke to find a vessel filled with an exotic amber liquid placed at the center of his table. Beside it was a letter:

> *Drink and follow the* shih, *the path of revelation. Discover the* qian ku, *the courage of kings of the Golden Age who were tested on mountain tops among white tigers and merciless storms. The flowing water will be your guide.*

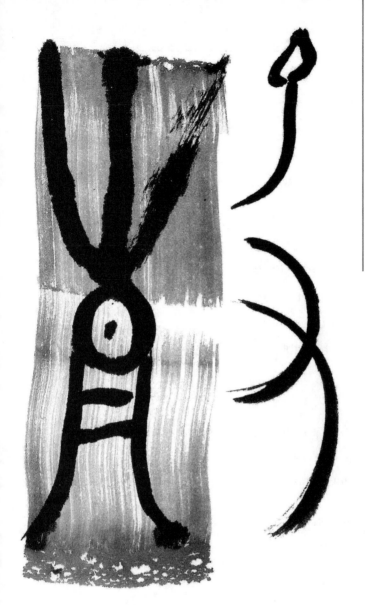

Drum (*Gu*):

When the moon was full, music echoed from the mountaintop. "*Da gu*," said Hu. "The drum is the First Sage of music." Cloaked in darkness, the instrument is displayed on its stand, a musician poised above it (left). The light area depicts a drumstick and a hand.

That night Hu rested on a bed of leaves beside the stream. Cautiously he removed the lid from the strange vessel and drank its fragrant ambrosia. Warmth radiated through his body. Pacified by a sensation of well-being, he stared absently at his lamp until its oil was nearly exhausted.

"Behold the trees," a voice commanded.

The startled Hu gazed into the darkness. Flocks of birds, luminous against the sky, stared down at him. Were these the same birds which by day perched in his windows sills? He was fascinated by the perfection of their colors.

M u s i c (*Yue*):

Many characters described musical instruments, but Hu searched for a new one. One night *Jen* whispered, "Music is the mother of the word and twin to the heart." Hu composed a left-facing *qi* with dot at the center to suggest the sun.

"Who speaks to me?" he whispered.

The outline of a woman's face rose from the mist.

"I am *Jen*, a spirit sent to guide you." (*Jen*: benevolence, first of the four virtues said by Confucius to be innate.) "You are steadfast and carry *hsin*. As a devoted archer seeks the heart of his target, fly to the *ming*. Follow the unity of *qi*."

The birds fluttered from the branches and gathered around him. Their feathers were like perfect brush strokes.

Again *Jen* spoke: "The receptive embraces the creative, thus all movement

Poetry (*Shi*):

Hu sought to simplify word and temple, which for centuries were joined in a maze of calligraphic strokes meaning "poetry as worship through words" or "words from the temple." Using the symmetry of his newly created music, he streamlined temple (top third of the character) and included basic elements of the pictogram.

comes to be exactly as it should be. In this lies the greatness of the earth. Heaven's law has an inner light that must be obeyed."

"*Tian na!*" Hu exclaimed. "Once I knew great power. Why have I ignored the presence of the small?"

In the days that followed, the Three Rivers of Chinese life would be revealed in ways he could not have imagined. Clearly the cares and tribulations of the plains did not count for much in the mystical world of Zhongnan Shan. Cosmology, philosophy, science: all

Valley (*Gu*):
The caoshu character represents mountain peaks spiraling downward to an open plain. Hu's mind became open and "empty" as the valley to receive new knowledge and wisdom.

seemed transient as those who had created them. Only the mountain remained
immutable. Here, removed from society,
humbled by sweeping vistas, the ancient
masters practiced their art and sought the
voice of Tao. Indeed, those who heard the
whispers and used the brush to manifest
their devotion were rewarded by the
admiration of kings. Yet the great masters
cared more for bowls of wine than the
praise or wealth.

Hu laughed aloud as he reflected
upon the Emperor T'ai-tsung's infatuation

(*Tao*) :

The pictogram shows hair (upper oblique strokes) connected to a wise head (center figure with two inner strokes) combined with the curved bottom line "to go." Taken together, the character means "The Path of Virtue" or "The Way." When Confucius (521–479 BC) implored Lao-tzu to tutor him in "The Way", the sage fumed, "Stop being so arrogant! All your demands, your self importance and overwrought enthusiasm— none of this is true to yourself. I have nothing more to say!" Confucius later remarked, "What to do with the dragon I do not know. It rises on the clouds and the wind. Today I have met Lao-tzu and he is like the dragon."

with the talents of Ma Chou, the poet/cal-
ligrapher whose brush performed miracles.
It was rumored that before the temple bell
tolled the second hour, Ma Chou would
consume seven bowls of wine and compose
The Twenty Desiderata with unerring
accuracy.

Three times T'ai-tsung sent his
generals to fetch the famous reprobate to
the Palace. They found Ma Chou snoring in
the rear of Madame Wang's dumpling
shop. Three times they spoke in the
name of the Emperor and three times
Ma Chou refused to budge. A verse by a

(F u):

These talismans of good fortune are found in homes, offices, temples, official buildings, and are carried on one's person. Often composed by Taoist priests, these magical improvisations are based on Chinese characters and are thought to expel evil demons. *Fu* means happiness. Hu's early struggles were lightened when he discovered a talent for *fu*. "Indeed, they quell inhibition," he wrote.

Court historiographer recalls the Emperor's desire:

> Indeed, on three successive occasions the summons came to call him,

> So great the Imperial love for men of worth and talent.

> If only every Court were so to regard its servants

> Where should we find a hero languishing in the wilderness?

Three Fruits of Plenty
(*shou, fu, lu*):

The peach, pomegranate, and bergamot (or Buddha's hand) symbolize long life, lots of children, and abundant wealth. Seldom seen outside of China, the characters appear easy to compose. They are not! Failed attempts littered Hu's dwelling. "Are the spirits angry?" he grumbled. Jen answered his question in a dream. "Simplicity gives no shelter to the false," she said.

Hu understood that his own
master, like T'ai-tsung, allowed no waste.
Indeed, not even the great Ma Chou was
allowed to squander his gifts. At last, the
soldiers carried him to Court.

Spirit (*Gui*):

The disembodied *Gui* floats through space, weightless and free. The curved tail represents a vortex of air caused by the spirit's movement. To avoid offending the dead, Hu was reluctant to alter the standard script. In today's China, the character means ghost or demon.

*A*utumn came with invigorating beauty. Wind sang in the branches. Rain whispered a thousand voices. The dialogues of forest creatures silenced Hu's own voice.

Warmed by a fire in a circle of stones, he practiced with the brush until sleep overtook him. The spirits visited as he slept, leaving behind new gifts. Though he had grown used to these visitations, he was startled one night by a shrouded figure filling the entire space beneath his lintel; it searched him with glowing eyes, and at last a voice rumbled out of the gloom: "Mind is golden thread. Yet gold is heavy and slows the step. The calligrapher leads by wanting nothing for himself, just as the universe lives forever because it does not live for itself."

Moon (*Yue*):
The crescent moon turns toward earth, bestowing positive energy. "The moon is a woman," Magu said. "She is home to spirit-beings of the ages." Indeed, Hu lamented, "she has cast a spell on me." Magu smiled at the love-struck *moshi*. "Poor mortal," she sighed. "One day he will know his spell is of his own making." The shaded pictograms (lower right) are old as China itself.

Hu thought he must be dreaming. When he awoke the next morning, he found exotic ceramic pots standing next to his brushes. He recognized the Irrawaddy black pottery of India. Inside were marvelous pools of ink: indigo, crimson, and black liquids with flecks of gold and silver.

The following night as he watched a lunar eclipse, the strange presence which had given him the wondrous inks spoke again: "Once these pots were void. Now they are filled with magic, just as the great valley is void yet always filling with new life. Be empty as the valley."

Emptiness as Art (*Xu*):

Emptiness is an art within art for the Chinese. Untouched spaces are integral parts of the work: "Living energy," Hu called them, reflecting Lao-tzu's philosophy of "non-action which leaves nothing unacted." Unpainted areas evoke infinite possibility.

Hu looked everywhere but could not find the shrouded figure, but the lingering words inspired him to compose "Emptiness as Art," its lines sinewy and surprising. Delighted by the success of the composition, his determination rose to the level of passion.

He became increasingly prolific. Fresh scrolls of poetry copied from the masters covered every space. His dwelling became a forest of imagery. He loved waking to find his scrolls fluttering from the ceiling. They cheered him and fueled his courage.

S p e a k (*Yan*) :

A mouth (bottom) beneath a roof, implying honorable words. Snatching a stem from a fir tree, Hu bound its leaves to create a writing tool symbolic of his resolve: "As the tree is without falsehood, so my brush is pure."

He copied the poems of T'ao Ch'ien. Like Hu, the poet had abandoned a post at Court to live a hard life on the land. Inspired by his lyricism, Hu composed his first poetic scroll:

The days grow short.

Yin and Yang struggle

In the fleeting sunlight.

On the distant mountains

Gathering snow gleams.

The great heroes of old

Are yellow dust forever now.

Such are the affairs of men.

Yet the Tao is infinite.

Lunar Eclipse
(*Yue shi*):

Moon (*yue*) floats above the character to eat (shi): the moon is being eaten. In Chinese mythology, the evil star *Luohou Xing* consumes the moon and threatens the domain of its goddess, Chang-O: A dark portent for mankind. For the spirits of Zhongnan Shan, however, it was a time to celebrate. Hu wrote: "I raise my cup and invite the moon down from the sky."

*A*s he meditated along the banks of the stream on a winter afternoon, Hu was startled to see a woman fishing through a hole in the ice. He attempted to speak to her but words failed him. The woman laughed at his awkwardness.

"I am Magu," she informed him.

For nearly a year, Hu had not seen another human being. Was Magu flesh and blood? Her fingers were long and noble, her body impossibly thin, her presence subtle as wind in high grass. A smile fluttered on her curving lips; blossoms glowed in her hair. She spoke of the stream.

"It is always new, enchanted as Zhongnan Shan itself," she told him. "To open the temple of the soul is to become as the stream." Slowly turning away, she whispered in a sly voice, "I hope you catch a fish."

Her beauty haunted him. She took up residence in his dreams. Each morning he searched for her along the banks of the stream. Indeed, to catch a fish was good fortune, yet capturing a single glance of Magu was priceless.

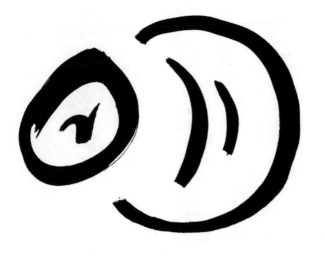

Brilliant, Enlightened (*Ming*):

The Chinese combine sun and moon (left to right) to produce the ideograph. Centuries after Hu's sojourn in Zhongnan Shan, the Ming Dynasty was famous for its art, literature, and orderly government. The dynasty also produced the "Three-Character Classic" (*San-tzu Ching*), which proclaimed human nature as fundamentally good, a stumbling block for Western missionaries preaching original sin.

The memory of her infused his hand with resolve. He created unique uses of space using the fastidious brush strokes of *kai shu* everyday script. It was a demanding discipline. And as if to recapture her essence, he purified his brushes in the stream, patted them dry on silk, and curled the bristles to a fine point with his lips.

With patience he mixed the liquids in the Indian pots with the thick powder of his ink sticks. His words shone on the paper with the glow of polished obsidian.

Justice (*Yi*):

Modern China uses the elegant three-stroke character (bottom) in everyday life. During the T'ang, however, justice was a combination of oneself, spear, hand, and sheep: A spear in an aggressive hand is subdued to right conduct like the docile sheep. Hu's Caoshu image (above) is used today by Chinese artists and calligraphers.

When the snows came and the distant glaciers increased, Hu warmed himself by practicing with the heavy wolf-hair brush. Slowly his strokes gained boldness. He composed many versions of "Harmony," wind suspended above water. Because wind is the ultimate master of water, its lines revealed the greater authority. The ever-changing water suggested unknown depths. Perhaps Magu waited for him in that unseen realm.

More often now the brush obeyed his will. Indeed, he was confident Xi would gain his prize: a unique calligraphy

Water Flows Swiftly Over Rocks Down the Mountainside: Hu's first scroll reflects meditations on the stream. His image combines (top to bottom): water (*shui*), flows (*liu*), swiftly (*jie*) over rocks (*shi*) down the mountain-side (*han*).

irresistible to the Emperor. He composed
a poem of resolution:

> To amass wealth in office is dubious
> honor,
>
> Nor is there hope of living long
> past seventy.
>
> When you are gone, who preserves
> your fame?
>
> Accept your gifts, content yourself
> with little.
>
> In the end, art and the word
> remain
>
> To remind us of the reality of the
> multitudes.

Kingdom (*Zhou*): Hu labored over the three-river pictographic rooted in the kingdoms of *San-Kuo*. The composition, which also means continent, revealed his artistic imperfections.

*I*n spring of his second year, when ice had retreated from the stream, again Magu appeared before him. The sight of her took his breath away.

Overwhelmed, Hu blurted out, "Magu, may I touch you?"

"You do not have the power," she laughed. "And even if you did, it would fill you with selfish desire. Your spirit would suffer."

"Ah, but I am lonely and the sight of you inflames me."

Earth (*Tu*):

China's "Three Character Classic" names water, fire, wood, metal, and Earth as universal elements. The top horizontal stroke is the Earth's crust; the lower horizontal is subsoil; the vertical line symbolizes all things growing from the subsoil. At lower right is one of the earliest Earth symbols

Magu lifted her fishing line from the water and held up a glistening, wet hook.

"I tell you as a courtesy that it is good to catch a fish. It is not so good to act like one," she smiled. "Your mission carries its own reward: *qian xu.* "

Qian xu: modesty. The great virtue of Chinese life. The soul of Confucian thought. How foolish he had been to flaunt his scholarship and challenge the wisdom of his elders. *Qian xu* must be his true mantra.

Beauty of Action
(*Mei Wei*):
The Caoshu characters
beauty (top) and action
echo the Tao's vision of
spiritual motion.

Hu turned as a branch fell in the forest.

In that instant, Magu vanished.

Days and nights blended as one. Hu slept little and ate less. He grew thinner. In the summer of his third year he chanced to see his reflection in the stream. He no longer recognized himself. How could he have changed so dramatically? For a moment he missed the old Hu, and in the next instant he released the feeling of loss. Transformation brings divine peace.

Oneself (*Zi*):

A nose (top right) was thought to be the beginning of human development in the womb. Another meaning comes from the tale of a wanderer who wished to see the gods before he would follow the Tao. After many years of searching, he found an ascetic in the Himalayas. "Do the gods really exist?" he asked. "Sit and close your eyes," replied the sage. The man did as he was told and was immediately enlightened. "Indeed," grinned the sage. "All answers are within you."

I have begun to vanish, he thought. "*Bian huan mo ce*. Man is a shadow and change unpredictable."

This realization astonished him, and with it came a new surge of freedom.

He composed characters which appeared to float above the paper like black butterflies. Others were dense as the earth itself, probing to its deepest reaches.

A written character, however abstracted, must hold together as a har- monious unit, and many forms of harmony

E y e (*Mu*):

In ancient times, the eye was drawn conventionally. It evolved for practical purposes into the character shown here. "The eye is a pathway to perception," Hu wrote. "But wisdom requires the entire self."

are possible. He rearranged the traditional lines of the "self," animating and abstracting the character with the fleeting spirit of the *Yi Ching*. He sought to capture the energy of the ceaseless reshaping of the universe. His characters spoke with many voices. Surely the combined characters of sun and moon would always mean "Bright," "Enlightened." Yet Hu's arrangement of them suggested more subtle meanings.

The inherent beauty of the characters and the grace of calligraphic

Face (*Mian*):

An important character, face reflects one's status and reputation. Face contains the eye enclosed in self, the connection to the cosmos drifting above it. "One's face must be strong as the plum flower," Hu's mother told him. "It blossoms even in the hardships of winter."

improvisation humbled him. He wrote in his journal: *I can not claim this work. It's magic springs from a deeper well.*

He became more adventurous. Indeed, he composed characters so swiftly that drops of ink flew from the tip of his brush and created pleasing abstractions. His injured right hand no longer resisted his efforts. His brush danced. It sang. At last, his calligraphy was pure joy.

Beard (*Xu*):

Three hairs drifting in space: a sign of maturity. Hu lamented his inability to grow a beard. "When you are older and responsible for a family, your face will sprout honor to your chin," Magu teased.

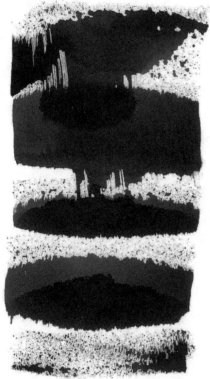

*T*hree years had passed. The blossoms of Summer descended upon Zhongnan Shan. The air was fragrant, the water sweet.

He had come to the mountain filled with self-importance. Now he was empty. He understood that to be a medusa of the universe was to be guided by humility. The ancients had taught this lesson with a handful of rice. They showed the seeds to their students and told them that without planting there is no crop; without cultivation no harvest; without

harvest life can not be sustained; without humility, the seeds will not take root.

One morning while gathering berries, Hu was surprised to see a riderless donkey tied to a tree. Arrayed across the animal's back were pouches of rice, woven blankets, and water. A silk envelope was fixed to its neck. Inside was a letter from Xi Er Gong. He read the instructions of his master.

Xi's words told him matters of State had unsettled the Palace. The

Wife (*Qi*):

The character (below) shows a woman carrying a broom. The character (above) is Hu's transformed character. Despite implied subjugation, an ironic proverb tells the real story: "If man is head of the family, woman is the neck that turns the head as and when it wants."

Emperor required wise counsel. Hu was to return immediately to Cha' ang-an.

With a sigh, he gathered his belongings for the journey. As he made his way down the mountainside he recalled his anger when Xi had sent him away. "I will live each moment for the day of my return," he assured his tearful mother. Now the day had come, but there was no triumph.

Indeed, his heart was heavy as Zhongnan Shan disappeared behind him in the mist.

The Highest (*Gao*):
The character evolves from
a pictogram of a tower built
above a palace (below). *Gao*
also implies moral superiority.
After much experimentation,
Hu created the Caoshu image
(above).

*H*u was an odd sight as he passed through the South Gate of Ch' ang-an. His beard jutted from his cheeks like a swarm of angry bees. Tangled hair cascaded over his shoulders and spilled into the folds of his blouse. Children followed him and laughed at the shadowy figure.

"Old man," they taunted. "Hurry! The Emperor waits!"

At the entrance of the Imperial City he was surrounded by guards.

"Please send word to Xi Er Gong that Chu Shui Hu has returned to his service," he told them.

Age (*Ling*):
The character for teeth (above) joined with total (below). As one ages, teeth are lost. A Chinese proverb tells us, "Much wisdom is spoken by false teeth."

The guards roared with laughter. What business did a beggar have with an esteemed Minister? Hu reminded them that appearances often mislead, and after some discussion a soldier was sent to inform Xi.

Hu was welcomed with a banquet. Unfortunately he had little appetite. The splendor of the Court was disconcerting. The display of wealth and power made him slightly dizzy. He had not anticipated this reaction. It is said that wisdom is like a

To Fly (*Fei*):

Early pictograms show a crane in flight, wings extended, neck folded. Hu reduced the wings to two dots and modified the body and long neck. He also wrote a poem: "The crane stands on one leg/ Waiting for a fish./ How diligent it is. /To contemplate its flight/ Is worth ten thousand pieces of gold."

person running along a path, and in the presence of such vainglory, Hu understood the path had carried him away from the life he had once cherished.

In respectful tones, Xi informed him that his blind mother had gone to The Yellow Spring. Indeed, he was now alone in the world. The news touched Hu's heart but did not shatter it.

"Have you discovered the great virtue?" Xi asked after a while.

"In emptiness is the rejuvenating power," he replied. *"Qian xu."*

Bamboo (*Zhu*):

Bamboo is hollow and shows "no mind" (ego), symbolizing perfect conduct. It bends to the storm. And since no part goes unused, it is "China's generous friend," celebrated by artists, musicians, and calligraphers.

"The Little Frog has become wise," Xi smiled. "Success once filled you with the ways of *zi da*. Self-importance. As the eyes of your departed mother were blind to the world, you were blinded to the path. As her heart ached for her husband and sons, so your heart ached for praise. Now let us see what your hard work has come to."

When Hu displayed his scrolls, the Minister could scarcely believe his eyes. Hu's script was extraordinary. Here, at last, was the enchanting calligraphy he had hoped for.

Leader (Top-down): Oneself (*zi*), Body (*shi*), To follow (*zhi*). Twenty-five hundred years ago, the philosopher-general Sun Tzu wrote "The Art of War" in which he gave five essential qualities of leadership: wisdom, sincerity, benevolence, courage, strictness. "With whom lies the advantages derived from Heaven and Earth?" he asked. The answer forecasts victory or defeat.

In the days that followed, Hu's brush fashioned urgent messages to the Emperor. The scrolls were irresistible to the eye. The Imperial view was broadened and informed, and a dangerous political rivalry in the provinces was averted.

Hu was much praised and sought after, yet the accolades which had once turned his head no longer moved him. The world of the Palace had become transparent. His soul was a palimpsest upon which Zhongnan Shan had inscribed its vision of swaying bamboo, the sound

Tranquility (*An*): Woman beneath a roof reflects tranquility of the heart and the balance of universal energies (above). Hu wondered if a deeper harmony was attainable. Tao is the greater order, Magu told him. "But it will not warm your hands on winter nights."

of tiger deep in the night, Magu's teasing smile. Even when the Emperor himself honored Hu's art, the Little Frog wished only that his mother might have lived to benefit from his success.

Indeed, his reputation would not be falsely passed on.

What would become of him? He remembered the stream and the seeds in the current in spring. Did destiny guide them? Were the medusas of the universe like the seeds?

Stream (*Chuan*): The shallow stream wandered many *li* down the mountainside. Pondering its travels, Hu wondered if perhaps mankind was born on its mossy banks. Indeed, the stream is an ally of heaven; it renews great waters and mirrors the sky. He closed his eyes and hurled ink onto the paper, creating what the ancients called "visitations of the spirits." He finished the composition with three lines evoking the ceaseless flow of water.

He knew the answers. The path was clear. He had learned that answers sought by the heart come from the act of knowing itself.

Zhongnan Shan had become part of him. The mountain would bring him to his destiny.

Power of Heaven
(*Tian qi*):

"Heaven" drifts above "Greatest Power." This work was composed near the end of Hu's three-year apprenticeship. By now, his inhibitions had vanished, the brush obeyed his will, and his will obeyed the wisdom of Zhongnan Shan.